UPSYDOWN
CARTOONS OF
DORSET LIFE

LYNDON WALL

AMBERLEY

'Lyndon's drawings always make me smile, and for anyone living in the county, the Dorset connection gives them extra point and charm.' Editor of The Dorset Year Book

'An amusing snapshot of the quirky characters and vibrant community that make living in Dorset so special.' Editor of Dorset Life

'Lyndon's cartoons are very jolly and very Dorset.' Martin Clunes

'Lyndon's cartoons are eye-catching, entertaining and splendidly appropriate. He regularly reminds us that it is humour which makes the world go round, keeps our feet on the ground and curtails any tendency to think too much of ourselves.' Alistair Chisholm, Mayor of Dorchester

'Mr Wall provides jollity in a grim modern world. More power to his pen!' Sir Brian May

'As the occasional subject of Lyndon's illustrations, I appreciate the warmth and wit of his style though I'd prefer he made me look ten years younger.' BBC weather presenter Sam Fraser

'If you laugh at a cartoon of yourself, it says a lot about the perception and the kindness of the artist.' Julian Fellowes

'The Yetties cartoon inspired me to do a concert in Yetminster Church to raise money for the church.' Bonny Sartin/Yetties

'Lyndon mixes magic, talent and humour with every pencil line in genius fashion. Original and funny, his art cleverly blends cheekiness and charm in drawings that are the perfect foil for our human foibles.' News Editor of The West Dorset Magazine

First published 2024

Amberley Publishing
The Hill, Stroud
Gloucestershire, GL5 4EP

www.amberley-books.com

Copyright © Lyndon Wall, 2024

The right of Lyndon Wall to be identified as the Author of this work has been asserted in accordance with the Copyrights, Designs and Patents Act 1988.

ISBN 978 1 3981 1825 6 (print)
ISBN 978 1 3981 1826 3 (ebook)

British Library Cataloguing in Publication Data.
A catalogue record for this book is available from the British Library.

Origination by Amberley Publishing.
Printed in the UK.

Foreword

I first came across Lyndon's work when I was editor of a news magazine in North Dorset. The news editor and I felt his cartoons elevated our magazine to another level, and so when we started our own magazine, *The West Dorset Magazine*, we asked him to provide fortnightly cartoons for us – only this time we would come up with ideas which not only reflected current events at Westminster but related them to events happening in West Dorset. Lyndon has risen to the challenge in such fine style we now put his cartoons on all our front pages – it's become our brand. His fabulous depictions of our wild notions are 'the talk of Westminster', according to our MP!

His cartoons always make people chuckle – though Boris Johnson as a hog roast at Bridport Food Festival, with Jeremy Hunt ladling on the fat, provoked anger from some quarters, with one particularly offended punter emailing all our advertisers to draw their attention to our cartoon. Unwittingly, their ire caused more people to fall in love with our magazine and, in particular, Lyndon's brilliant cartoons.

Miranda Robertson
Editor of *The West Dorset Magazine*

Introduction

It has been tremendous fun drawing these cartoons. Some may be familiar to you, having appeared in various local publications, among them *The West Dorset Magazine*, *Dorset Life* and *The Dorset Year Book*. The cartoons, interspersed with caricatures of notable Dorset residents, past and present, offer a light-hearted view of the events and goings-on in the county since the end of 2021. Before that, the focus for all of us was on getting through the pandemic.

I am often asked if I am a whizz at computer technology. Absolutely not. The equipment is basic: mostly pens and colouring pencils bought from the children's section of high street stationers. On one occasion a few years ago this was nearly my undoing. I was booked as caricaturist at a high-end circus-themed party, tasked with drawing all sixty-five guests, young and old, during a three-hour stint. My host thoughtfully positioned me outside the big top next to a roaring brazier, which was fine – until my pencils melted!

My art teacher at school was great, and supportive to the extent that he allowed me to sit at the back of the class and basically do my own thing. It was during this time that I gained my prized Blue Peter Badge, coming runner-up in their national painting competition (26,000 entries), and was taken on by an agent to produce hand-painted advertising signs for London department stores and greetings card illustrations.

What looked like a promising start to my art career took a sudden downward turn. My art teacher retired and I was back again under the restrictions of the curriculum. I started expressing myself more through music-making, and thanks to another inspirational teacher went on to pursue a successful career in music.

My artwork didn't stop altogether, although it did take a back seat. Back in the 1990s I used to provide black-and-white caption cartoons for several London journals using the old Letraset shading dots. It was only when an editor refused a batch of my cartoons, saying they wouldn't scan properly, that I decided to give that style a miss. About five years ago I got a lucky break with a newly launched Dorset magazine. This in turn led to drawing political and Dorset-themed cartoons for several more publications.

Coming runner-up in the national Ellwood Atfield Political Cartoon of the Year Awards 2022 was a surreal experience. The event was held at St John's, Smith Square, Westminster, attended by the great and the good in cartooning and politics. I was there, I thought, simply as an interested onlooker. Only when I was being congratulated on stage by Angela Rayner and Jacob Rees-Mogg did I realise that I should have been preparing a speech rather than sketching the old pipe organ at the back.

Which brings me to the advice I received many years ago from no less a personage than the political cartoonist of the *Daily Mail*: persevere – a good tip for us all.

I hope you enjoy the cartoons in *Upsydown*, a reminder of just how much goes on in our beautiful and not-so-sleepy county of Dorset.

Lyndon Wall
Blandford, Dorset

Lord Fellowes of West Stafford, eminent among Dorset men.

Flameburst, Verwood's annual fireworks display at The Fuzzy Bit. Then Chancellor Rishi Sunak's Budget speech warns of 'difficult times ahead', while William Shatner, at ninety, is the oldest person to have rocketed into space.

Dorchester gets council backing to bid for city status in Elizabeth II's platinum jubilee celebrations the next year.

The Dorset locals can't resist carolling on Gold Hill, Shaftesbury.

Prime Minister Boris Johnson's popularity is at an all-time low, even within his own party. North Shropshire, a Tory safe-seat for 200 years, is lost to the Lib Dems, while Liz Truss is possibly making a move for the leadership. None of which seems to concern the Dorset locals.

In the news this week, the Dorset Knob Throwing and Food Festival, scheduled for May Day, is cancelled – not as a result of Covid, but because of its increasing popularity (8,000 attended back in 2019).

While Boris faces a Met investigation over the Partygate scandal, West Dorset MP Chris Loder treats us to a dose of 'proper politics'.

Jackie Weaver shot to fame when the Handforth Parish Council meeting she chaired went viral in 2021. Here I have imagined the unflappable 'Queen of Calm' visiting the county.

After a gap of ten years, Christchurch again has its own town crier.

SWR is back on track, restoring a full train timetable for Dorset residents. Here, making the most of the facility, are Dorset's eight MPs.

Dorset's Ridgeway Singers and Band, led by Tim Laycock and Phil Humphries, are renowned for performing the songs and carols of old Dorset. Here they are offering 'Tea with William Barnes' at The Exchange, Sturminster Newton.

The Dorset Rural Music School in Blandford, the last of its kind in the country, offers musical tuition on any instrument, as well as choral and orchestral opportunities, for young and old alike. For many years it was run by the eminent musicologist Dr Richard Hall.

Russia invaded Ukraine in February 2022. The good folk of Blandford, as elsewhere, are quick to respond with aid.

The response in West Dorset is equally overwhelming. Bridport is receiving donations at the red telephone box in South Street.

A poignant sight in Stourpaine: the Tommy Soldier silhouette draped with the Ukrainian flag.

Publican and local hero Tom Littledyke loads donations onto his minibus in Lyme Regis for a return trip to war-torn Ukraine.

Our beloved Thomas Hardy in 'Casterbridge'.

The Dorset locals embrace the principles of permaculture.

An April Fools' Day cartoon, announcing the imminent pedestrianisation of Dorset. The setting is Sturminster Newton.

A bizarre incident makes local news headlines. A prisoner escapes from police custody in Poole wearing just his underwear. After an extensive search he is eventually picked up in Bournemouth.

The then Prince Charles is due to open the palatial new play park in Poundbury, Dorchester, hailed 'fit for a king'.

157 acres of farmland near Bere Regis, bought by legendary Queen guitarist and wildlife campaigner Brian May back in 2012, is gradually being restored to natural woodland to promote wildlife and is open to the public.

Early preparations are underway following the announcement that the eight-day Tour of Britain cycling race is due to pass through Dorset for the first time in its history.

May Day celebrations at Cerne Abbas. An early start is needed to see the Wessex Morris Men, in company with the Dorset Ooser, performing on the hillside next to the Cerne Abbas Giant.

"FARMER HITS BACK OVER 'DISAPPEARING' CHALK CARVING ROW"

Amid ongoing concerns over the state of the Osmington White Horse, the landowner speaks out, claiming that the landmark chalk figure of George III is fine, as it has been for the last 200 years.

The 'lost' village of Tyneham, deserted since the Second World War.

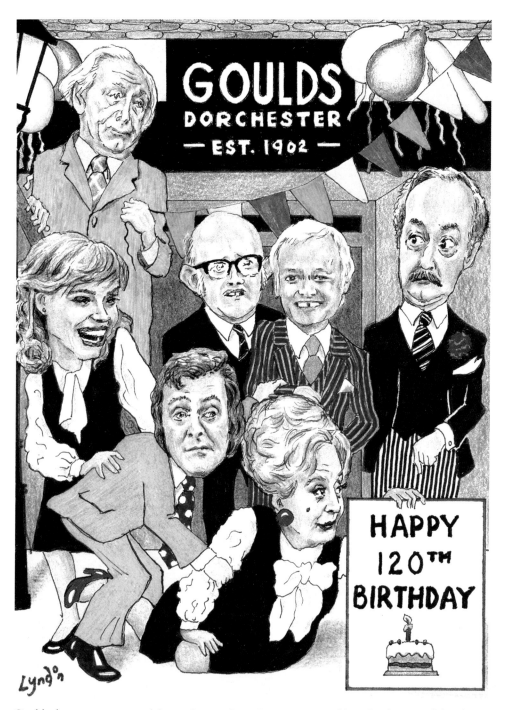

Goulds department store celebrates its 120th anniversary, assisted here by the cast of the classic sitcom *Are You Being Served?*

The popular Gold Hill Cheese Race is one of Dorset's newer traditions.

The then Prince Charles makes a surprise visit to the Royal Bournemouth Hospital.

Chris Loder MP is fighting to stop 'Norchester', the 4,000-home development just north of Dorchester, as is Alistair Chisholm, the award-winning town crier.

Our great dialect poet, William Barnes.

Preparing for the beacon-lighting ceremony, which marked the start of Elizabeth II's platinum jubilee celebrations. Pipers across the country were called on to perform a special commemorative tune to start the ceremony – in my case, on stage at the Blandford Railway Arches.

Dorset locals celebrate Elizabeth II's platinum jubilee in Wimborne.

The platinum jubilee celebrations on Burton Bradstock Beach. I thought I was being original depicting the Red Arrows flying overhead in this formation, only to see them doing it for real a few days later.

Boris hangs on by a thread. In the background is Durdle Door, near Lulworth.

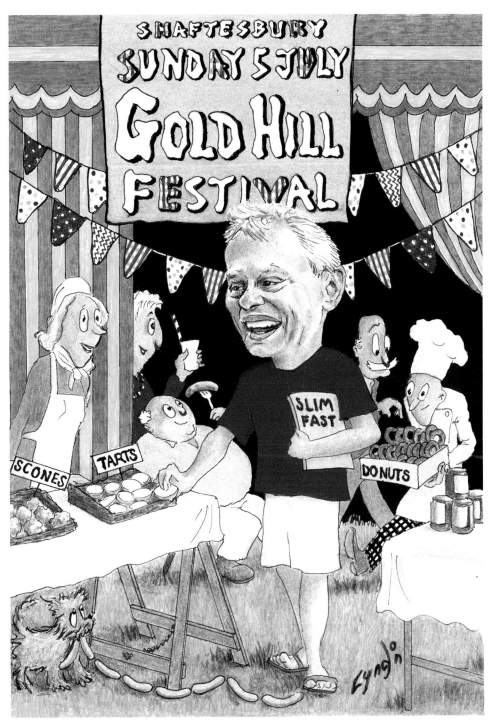

Martin Clunes, Dorset resident and champion of good causes, makes local news with his impressive dieting.

This is the much-talked-about hog roast cartoon of the then prime minister. Most people saw the funny side.

The Ashmore Filly Loo, an ancient Dorset celebration, takes place around the village pond on the Friday nearest Midsummer's Day.

A testing time for the trainee locomotive drivers at Shillingstone station.

The Dorset locals are spoilt for choice when it comes to village fêtes.

Shillingstone Railway holds its popular summer rally.

Archaeologists digging near Winterborne Kingston make an important discovery.

The Tolpuddle Martyrs' Festival. Quite a line-up.

Despite the summer heatwave, with the highest temperatures on record, Dorset's beaches are nevertheless crowded.

An American professor praises the quality of the sand on Weymouth Beach.

Holidaymakers are facing severe delays at Dover and Folkestone, due in part to a lack of French customs officers. Many are rebooking and travelling through Dorset to get to France and Spain.

BBC weather presenter Sam Fraser searches for her friends at Badbury Rings.

Some say that Henry Hoover (originally built in Beaminster) should be the new prime minister.

En route to the show.

A curious incident makes local news. A pile of clothes is discovered on Weymouth Beach, triggering responses from the emergency services. Through a mobile phone found among the items, the owner is traced to a nearby pub. But wearing what?

The drought situation in Dorset has become serious, with fires breaking out across open heathland, often through the careless use of disposable BBQs. Most supermarkets in the county are removing them from their shelves.

The weather is perfect, the show a resounding success.

Another of Dorset's ever-popular festivals.

A week to go, and there are likely to be additional challenges facing the competitors when they enter the Dorset Stage of the much-awaited Tour of Britain.

'A Remarkable Life'

Queen Elizabeth II

Elizabeth II passes away (Thursday 8 September), three days after Lizz Truss becomes prime minister. The Tour of Britain, as with most events, is cancelled. At this sad time, it was an honour to be asked to play the pipes at various locations around Dorset, including Gold Hill.

Fuel prices are at their lowest since mid-May, but households face crippling energy bills this winter.

Dorset's very own Olympic equestrian.

As part of a multi-million-pound project, twenty-two electricity pylons are being pulled down in Dorset's AONB, the cables running underground. Later this month, the *Flying Scotsman* steam train will visit Swanage Railway.

"GOD SAVE OUR GRACIOUS CLOCK"

THE YETTIES OF YETMINSTER

A fundraising campaign is underway to restore Yetminster's historic (1683) faceless clock – a good reason for imagining the much-loved Dorset folk group The Yetties (who had retired in 2011) busking for the cause.

Blackberry picking in Blandford is not without its challenges.

While Weymouth Pirate Fest attracts much interest locally, time for Liz Truss is fast running out.

Film producer and local landowner Guy Ritchie makes news headlines when he buys Compton Abbas airfield.

The Mayor of Dorchester, Janet Hewitt, and award-winning town crier Alistair Chisholm celebrate Halloween in Brewery Square.

It's Halloween, and actor Griff Rhys Jones stars in a locally made film set in Poole and Bournemouth.

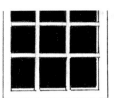

Larcombe's of Beaminster celebrates twenty successful years in the ironmongery business. The current owner, Simon Larcombe, looks pleased to be flanked by the two Ronnies, Corbett and Barker, and Trigger from *Only Fools and Horses*.

A woman from Salisbury claims to have photographed a ghost at Knowlton church, near Cranborne. The claim is disputed by experts.

Dorchester has good reason to celebrate the 100th anniversary of Howard Carter's discovery of Tutankhamun's tomb, and the Dorset locals relish an excuse for dressing up.

Simon Hoare MP looks set to break into a song and dance routine as the Boundary Commission proposes reassigning a large portion of West Dorset to his North Dorset constituency.

The Dorset locals venture beyond the county border following news that the A303 is to close while a temporary bridge is removed. The pothole fixer anticipates his services will be needed.

With severe flooding across parts of Dorset, Sir David Attenborough heads down to Weymouth for filming. Here I have imagined him asking directions from Stourpaine.

A stretch of the A31 is at last free of roadworks. At the same time, the misspelled Wimborne sign is replaced.

The build-up to Christmas proves challenging for many.

Merry Christmas from the Dorset locals, who are carolling in Child Okeford.

The famous Hardy Tree in London, surrounded by gravestones arranged by the young Thomas Hardy, topples after 180 years. The New Year Honours List sees Brian May knighted by King Charles.

BBC weather presenter Sam Fraser performs stand-up in Shaftesbury.

The West Dorset Magazine expands its readership to include Weymouth and Portland. A fun cartoon to draw, considering the time of year, and nice to feature Weymouth's famous Punch and Judy show.

With the current spell of bad weather, the poor state of Dorset's roads is highlighted.

After a century, Colehill Cricket Club is faced with having to end adult cricket due to complaints about balls landing in neighbouring gardens. Thanks to national media coverage and support from celebrities such as Ben Stokes, donations flood in to provide the necessary safety netting.

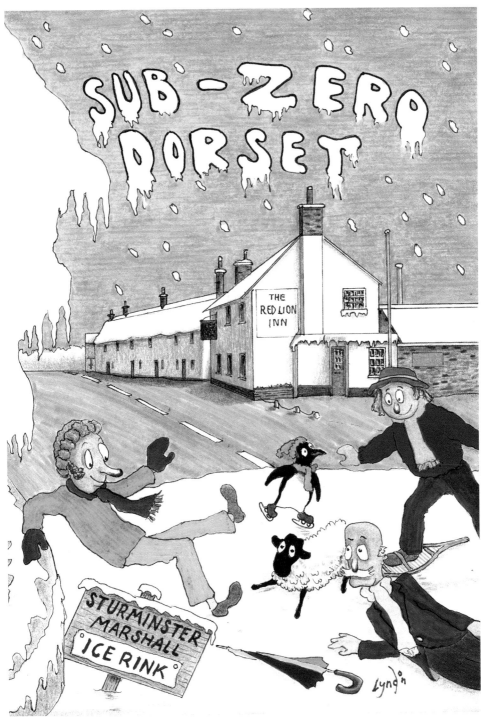

The New Year sees temperatures plummet in Dorset, as elsewhere, with severe flooding, ice and snow.

Steptoes of Bridport celebrates thirty years as an independent retailer selling high-quality footwear and clothing.

Amanda Pearson becomes the new Chief Constable for Dorset Police.

President Zelensky makes a surprise visit to the UK. After seeing King Charles and addressing MPs in Westminster Hall, he travels down to Dorset to meet Ukrainian troops training at Lulworth Camp.

The Upside Down House, a popular tourist attraction in Bournemouth, currently faces an uncertain future.

Hunting in Dorset. The foxes, protected by law, have little to worry about.

The staff of *The West Dorset Magazine* celebrate their recent crop of local and national awards.

Jay Blades, presenter of BBC's
The Repair Shop, makes national news
with the opening of his new furniture
shop in Poole.

The indefatigable Chris Loder MP continues to speak up for our local train service.

The government allocates a substantial fund (£2.9 million) for road repairs in Dorset. The long-suffering pothole fixer is grateful, as is Simon Hoare MP.

The good people of Portland voice their concerns over plans for a new waste incinerator. Dorset Council subsequently turns down the scheme.

A major oil spillage in Poole Harbour makes national news.

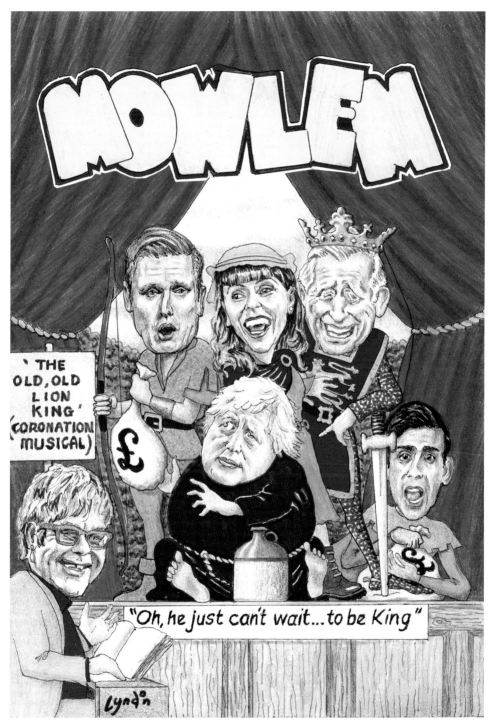

As King Charles's coronation date approaches, I imagined him heading an all-star cast, Robin Hood-style, at the Mowlem Theatre, Swanage.

The Dorset locals in good spirits outside Thomas Hardy's former home.

Charles III's coronation celebrations.

The former Second World War underground transmitter bunker on the Jurassic Coast near Weymouth, now used for holiday lettings – a great excuse to have the cast of *Dad's Army* in temporary residence.

The Boundary Commission's final decision on reshaping Dorset's constituencies baffles many, including the cast of the 1980s sitcom *Yes Minister*.

The site of the former council offices at Weymouth's North Quay is to become a temporary car park prior to redevelopment, an opportunity too good to miss for the *Blackadder* cast.

Protests break out at Portland amid controversy over the arrival of the Bibby Stockholm asylum seekers' barge.

Sherborne Abbey's first building redevelopment in a century will provide new toilet facilities and improved disabled access. Lending a hand here are Laurence Llewelyn-Bowen, Nick Knowles with his *DIY SOS* team, and local girl Carole, a contestant on *The Great British Bake Off*.

Ahead of the coming general election, a recent poll puts the West Dorset Lib Dems neck and neck with the Tories for the first time in 139 years, a source of entertainment for the cast of *The Vicar of Dibley*.

A prominent local figure, Peter Lush, author, composer and military historian, is chairman of the Society of Dorset Men.

With the long-running Post Office Horizon scandal exposed in a four-part ITV drama, former Yetminster postmistress Tracey Merritt is seen riding a pliosaur – its fossilised remains were recently unearthed on Dorset's Jurassic Coast and featured in a documentary by Sir David Attenborough.

About the Author

Lyndon Wall lives in Blandford, Dorset. A prolific, award-winning cartoonist described as having 'a razor-sharp wit wrapped in cottonwool', his cartoons are well-known across the county, regularly appearing in local publications, among them *The West Dorset Magazine*, *Dorset Life* and *The Dorset Year Book*. Lyndon is a member of The Cartoonists' Club of Great Britain, and was runner-up to *The Sun* in the national Ellwood Atfield Political Cartoon of the Year Awards 2022. He also plays the bagpipes.